ColorVER

Coloring Books for All Ages

Crazy Creatures

Vol. 1

MW00915683

Color VERSE
Color Testing Page

This coloring book features high-quality paper that is perfect for a variety of coloring mediums, including colored pencils, pastels, crayons, and gel pens. It is best to place a blank piece of paper or cardstock behind the page you are working on so you can color with confidence knowing that your masterpiece won't bleed through.

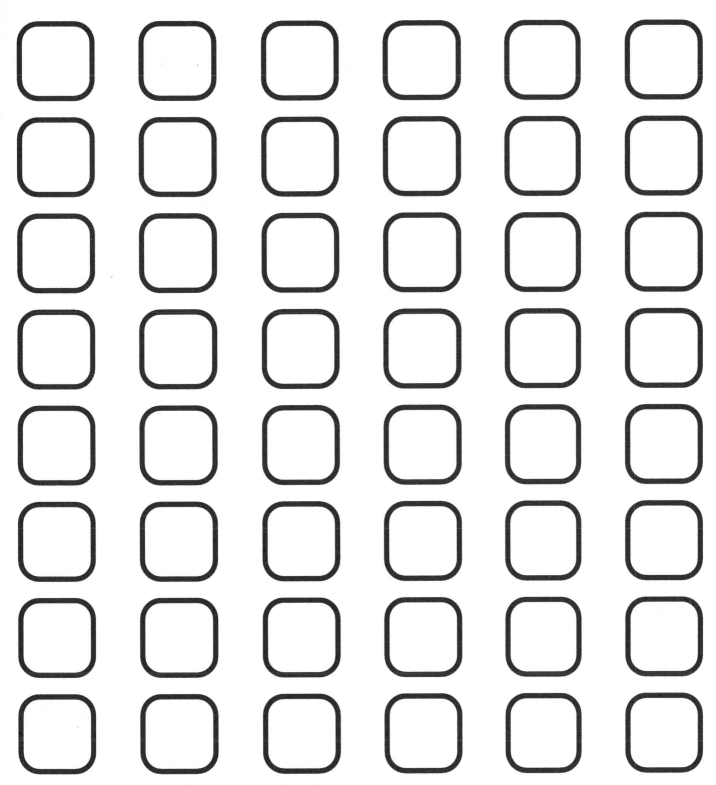

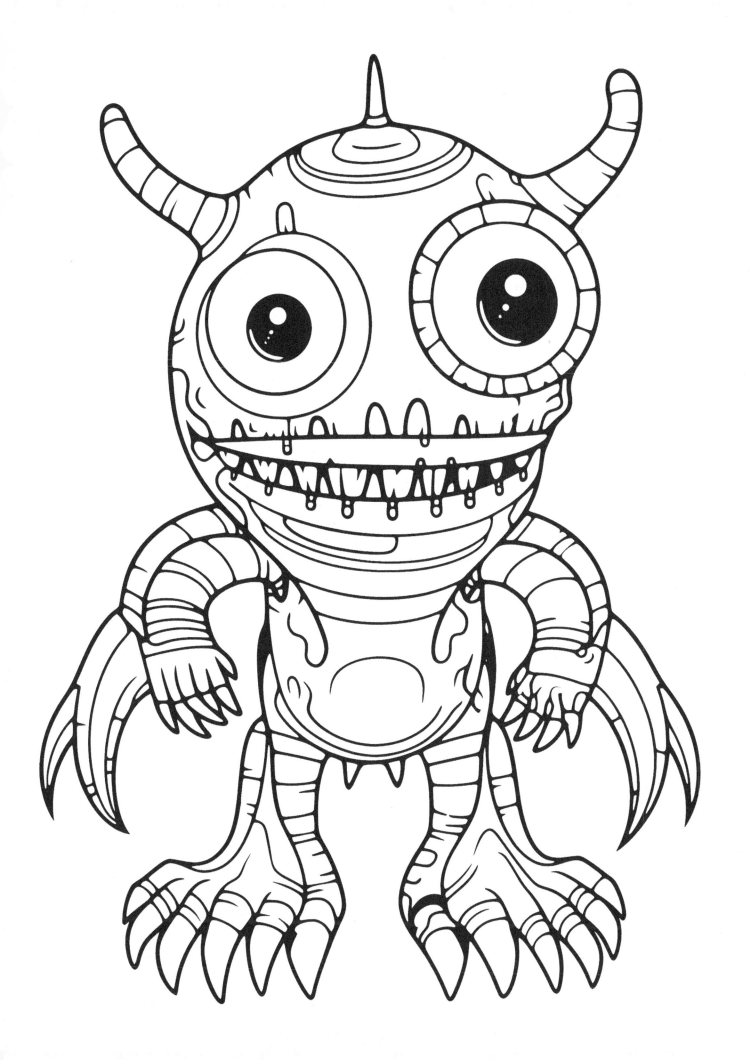

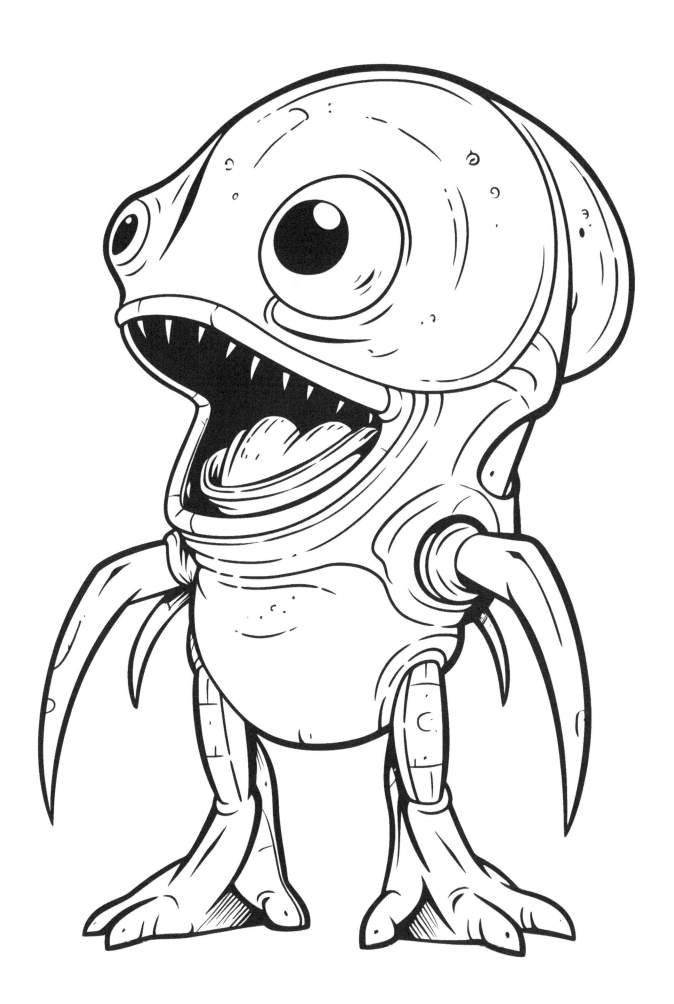

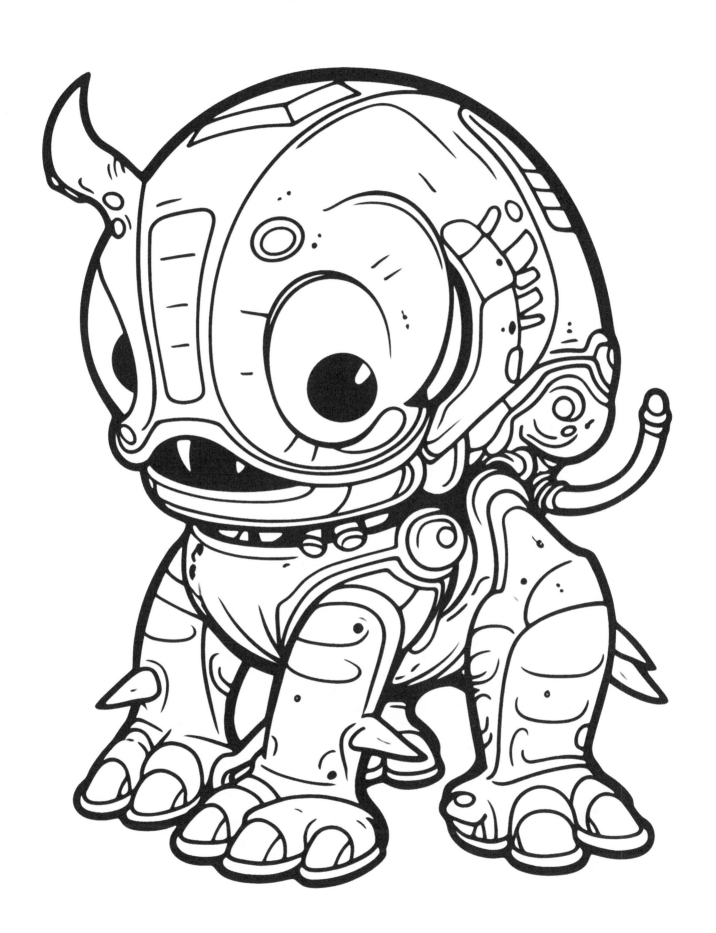

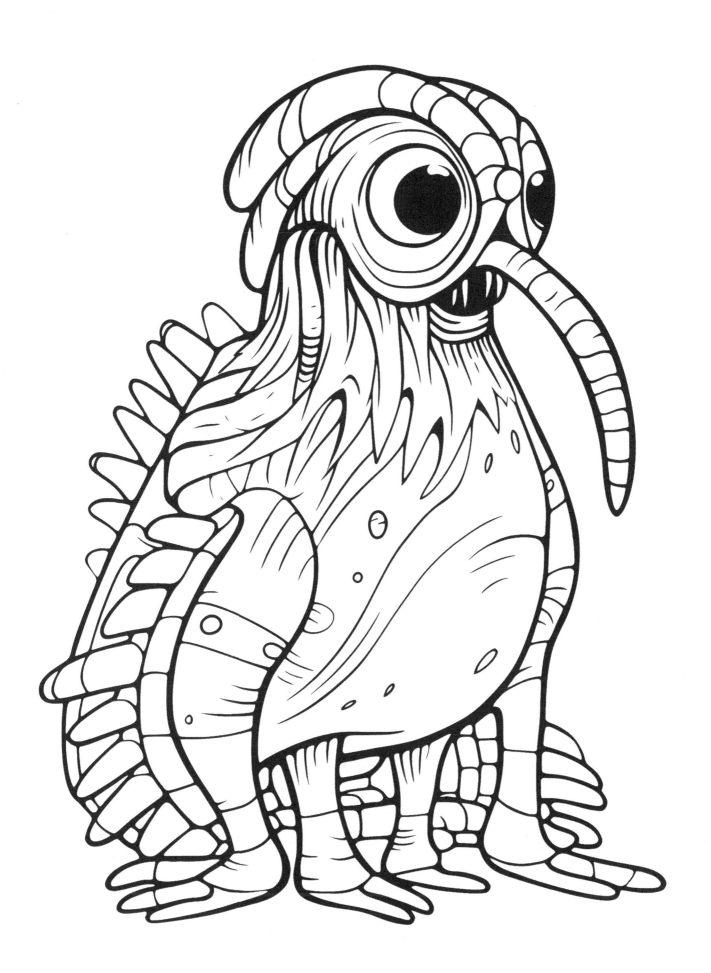

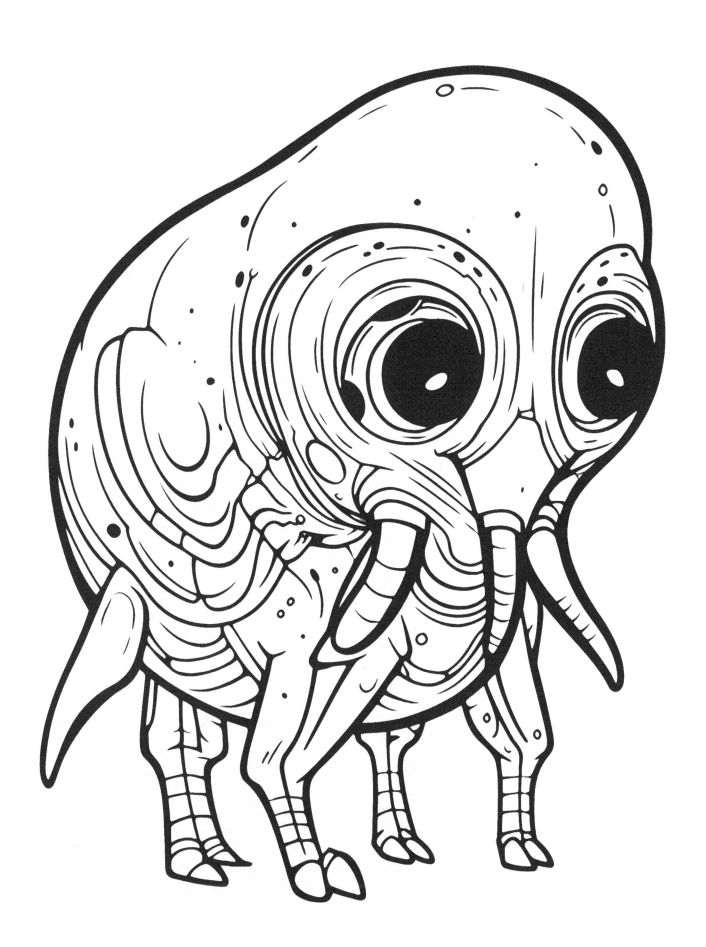

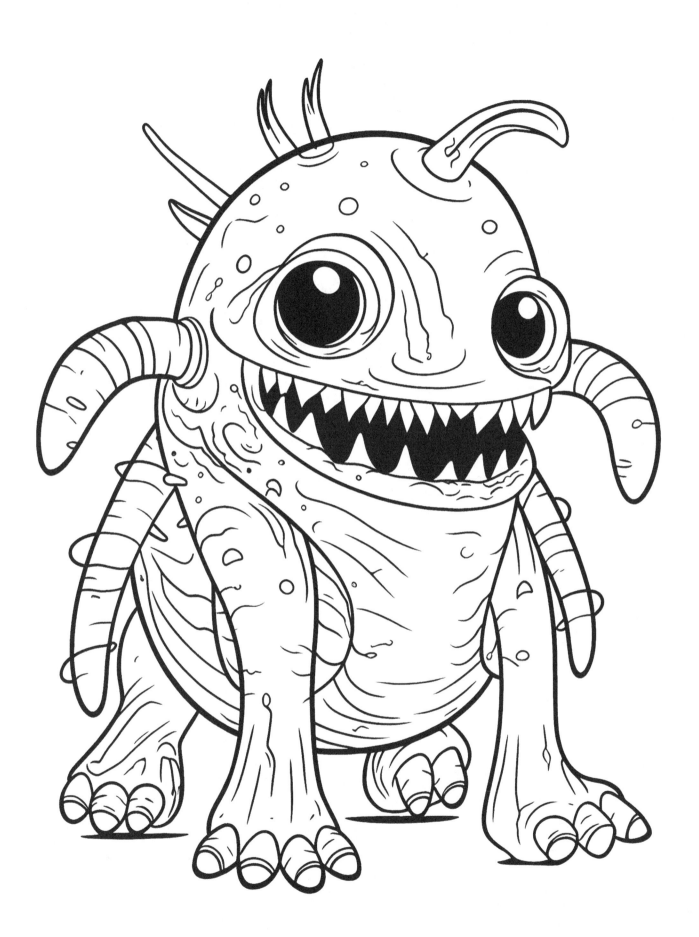

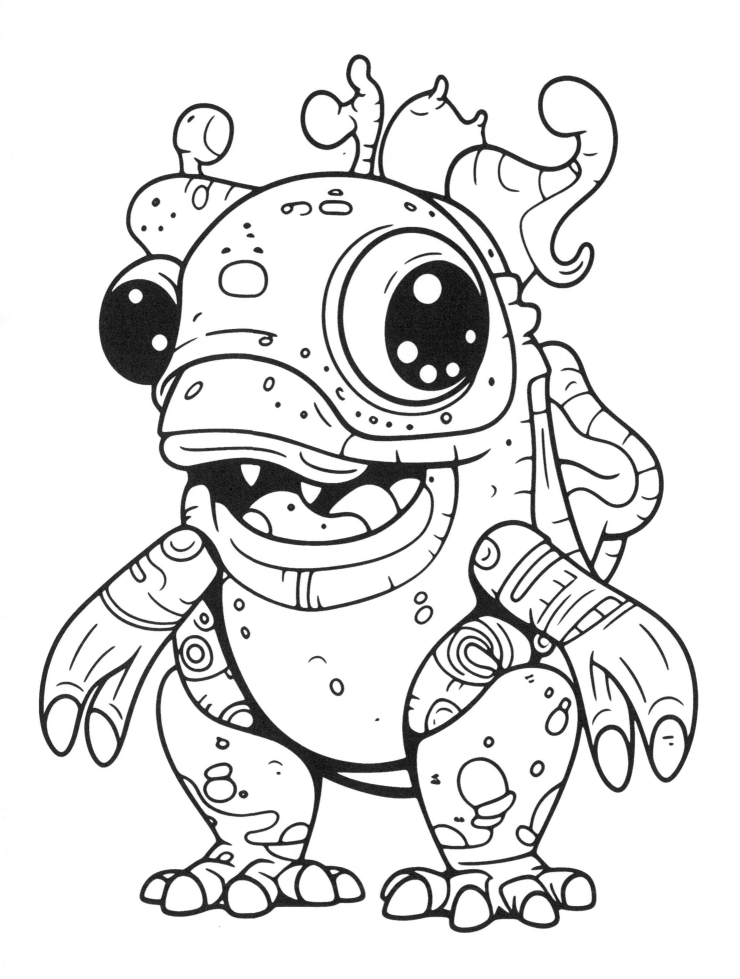

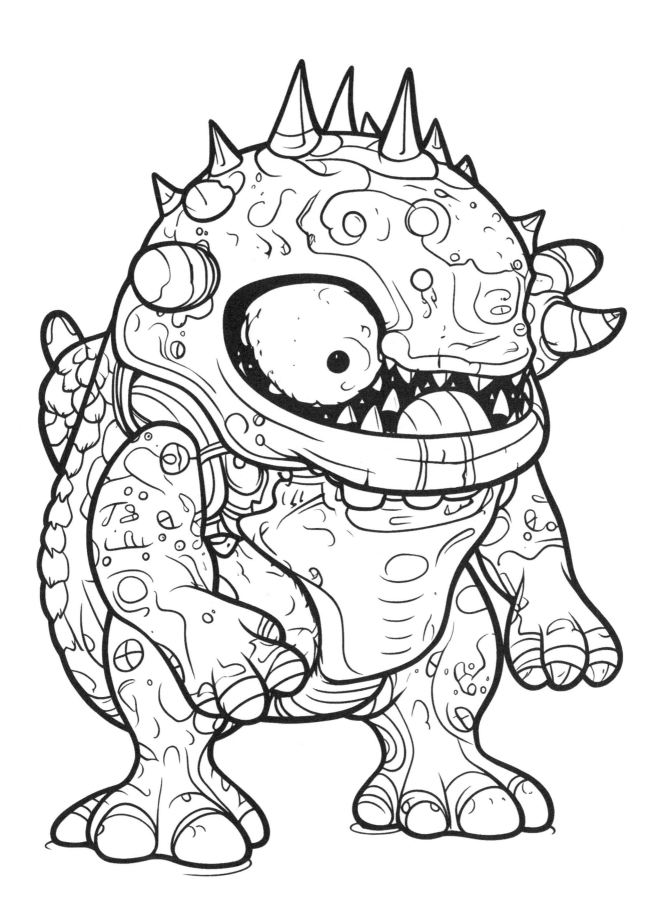

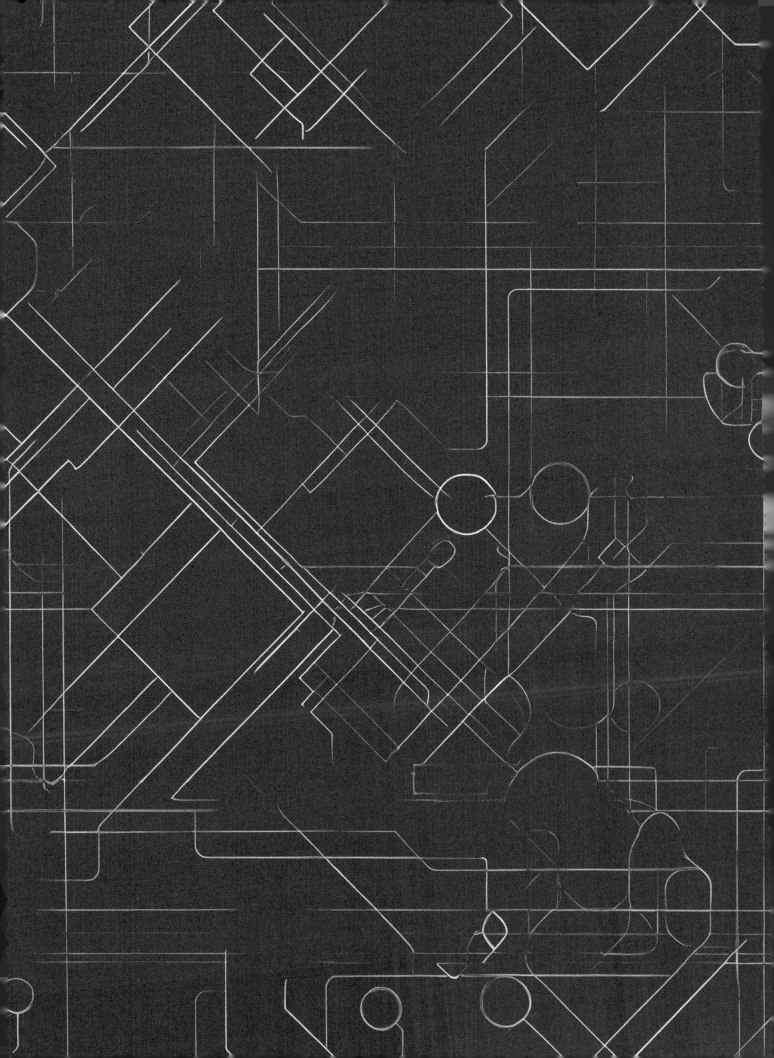

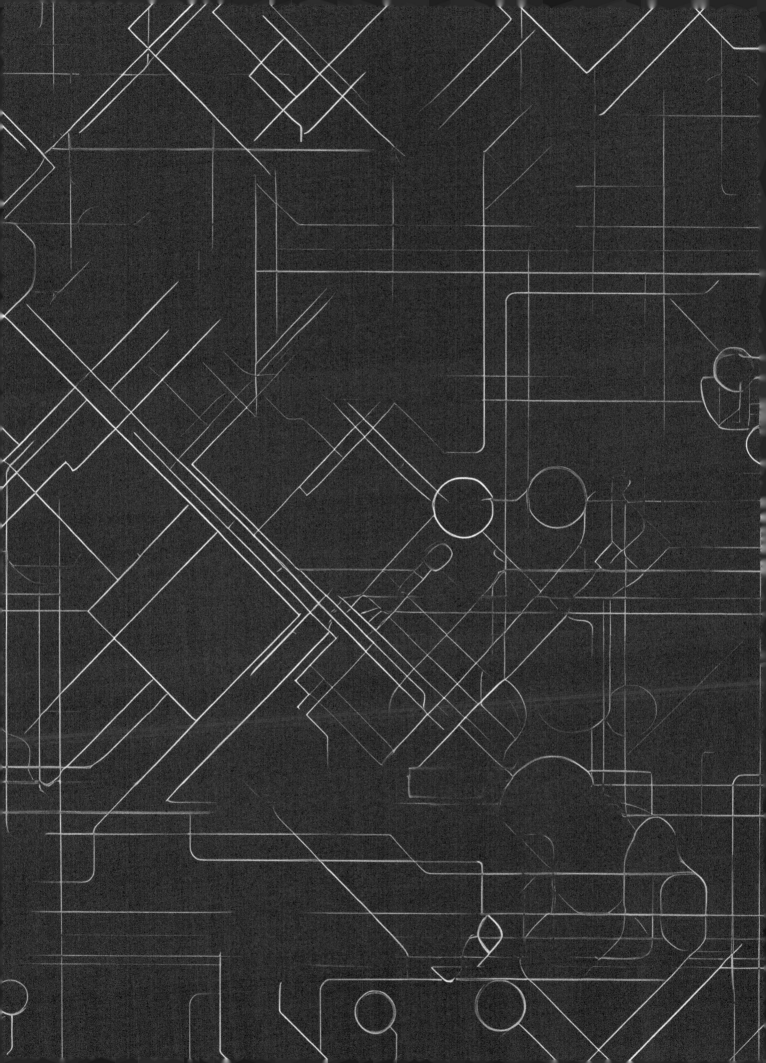

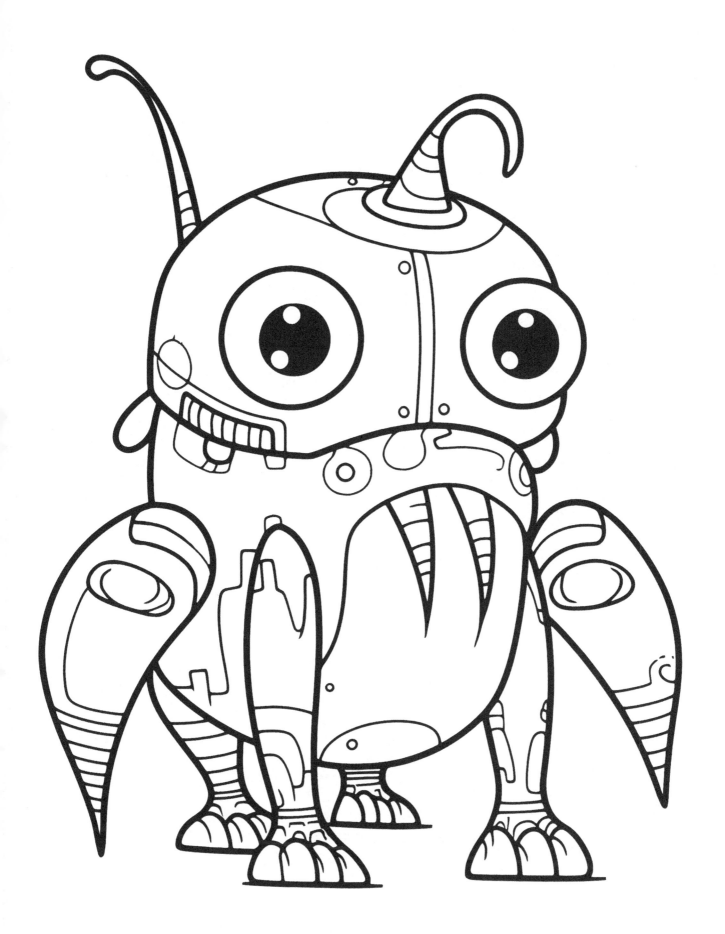

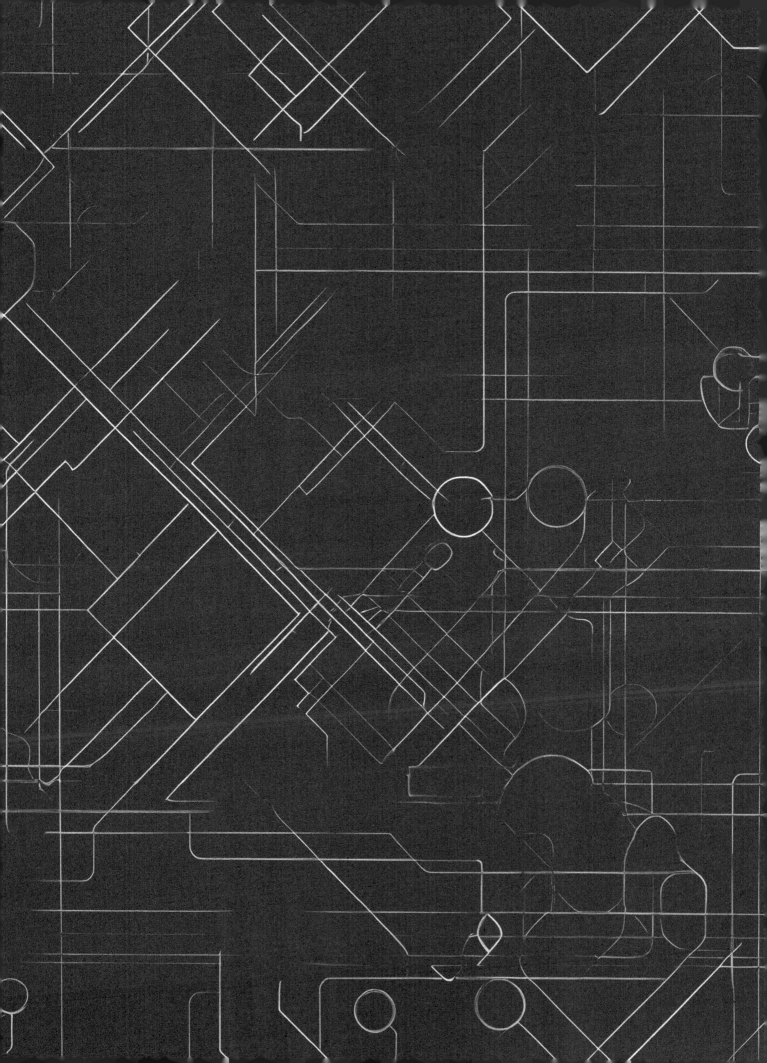

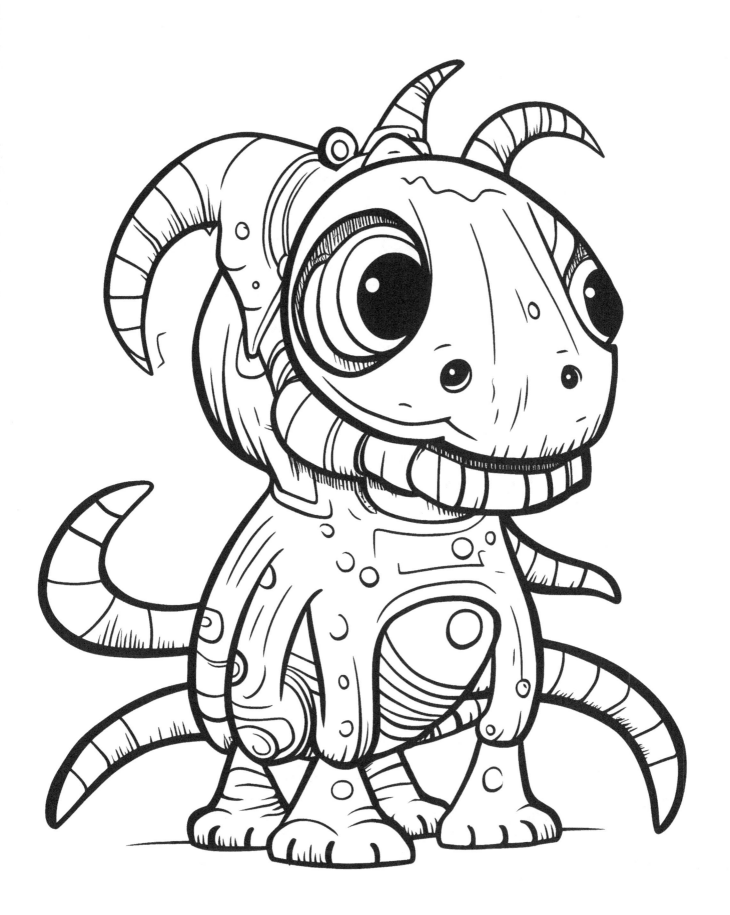

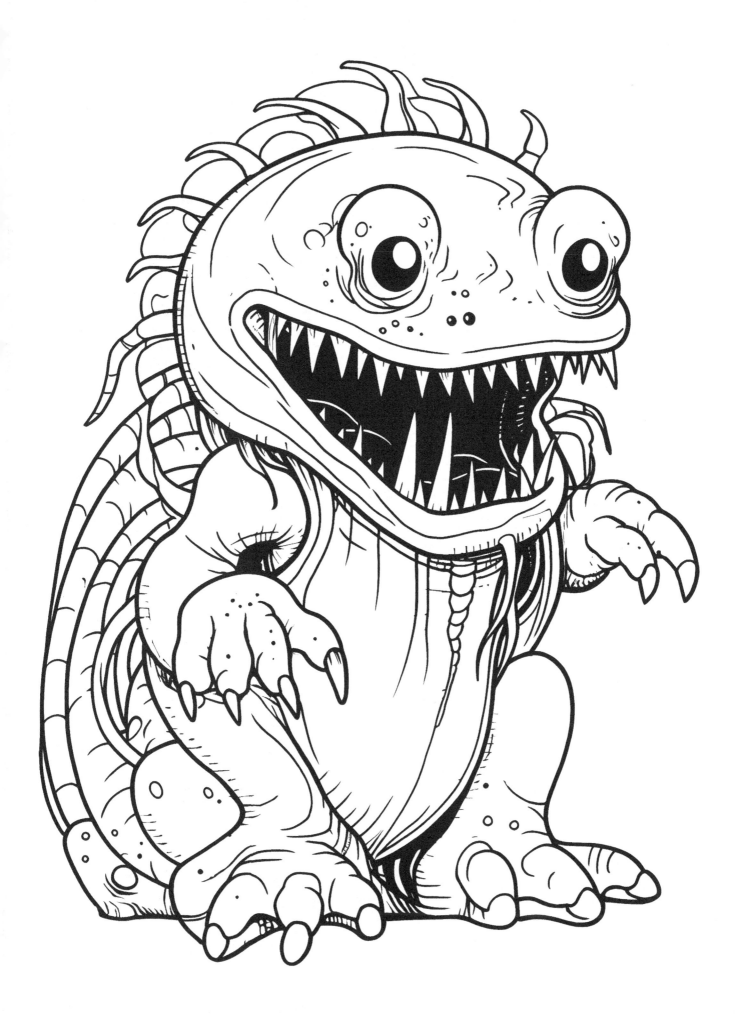

Made in United States
Orlando, FL
28 September 2023

37354020R00057